To Eleanor, Sophie,
Audrey, Chloe,
and Jack—
*a new generation of
adventure!*

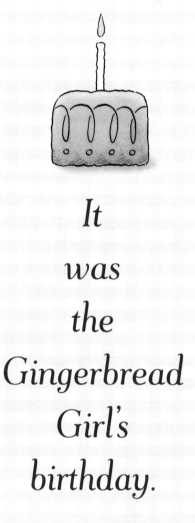

*It
was
the
Gingerbread
Girl's
birthday.*

To celebrate, the little old man and woman who baked her gave the Gingerbread Girl a gift tied with a licorice-whip ribbon to match her hair.

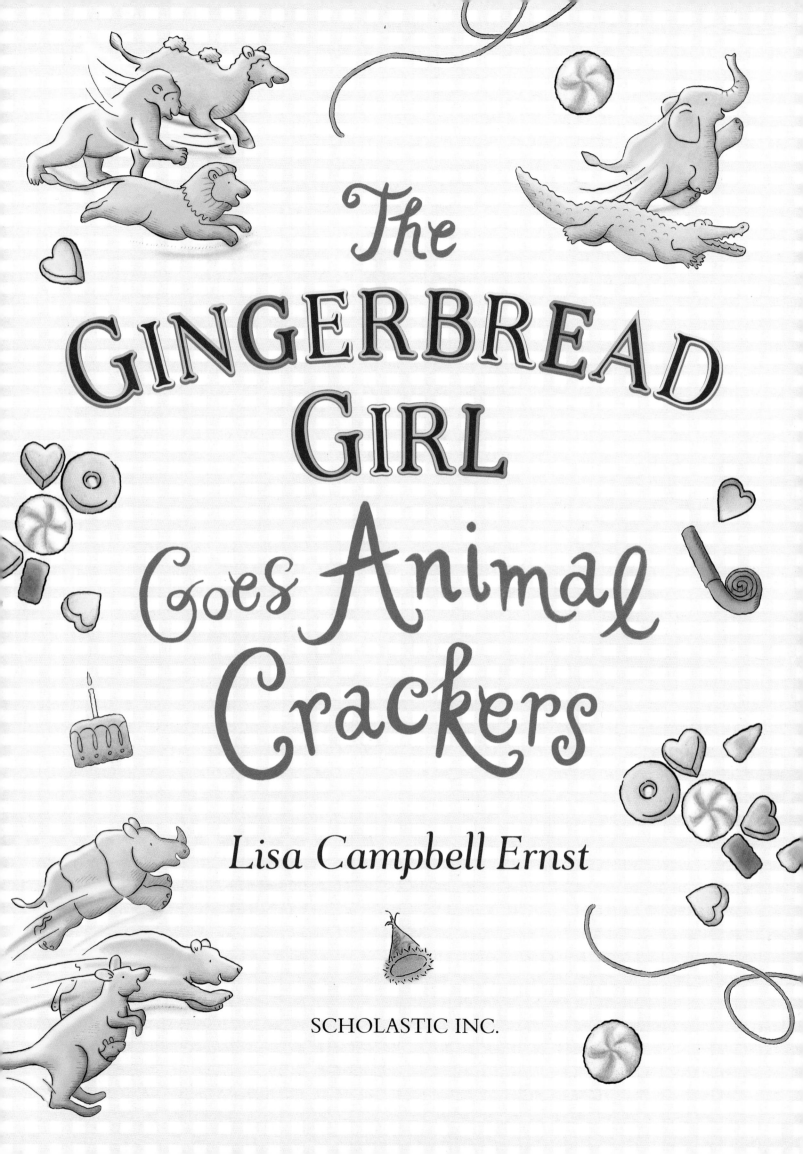

The GINGERBREAD GIRL Goes Animal Crackers

Lisa Campbell Ernst

SCHOLASTIC INC.

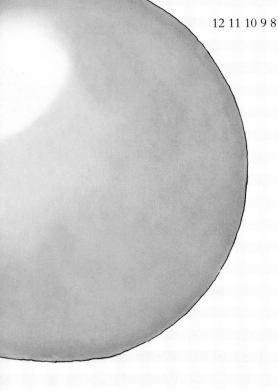

ISBN 978-0-545-53934-0

12 11 10 9 8 7 6 5 4 3 2   13 14 15 16 17 18/0

Printed in the U.S.A.   08

This edition first printing, January 2013

Only one year ago the Gingerbread Girl had outsmarted the same greedy fox that had tricked and eaten her brother, the Gingerbread Boy.

She sometimes still saw the fox lurking by the river, waiting to offer rides to other unsuspecting cookies. The Gingerbread Girl made sure to stay as far away as possible.

As the Gingerbread Girl began to unwrap
her birthday present, mysterious
grunts and growls came
from inside.

Sliding the paper off, she gasped. "Animal
Crackers! I've always wanted friends like me to
play with!"

Then the Gingerbread Girl carefully began
to lift the top ...

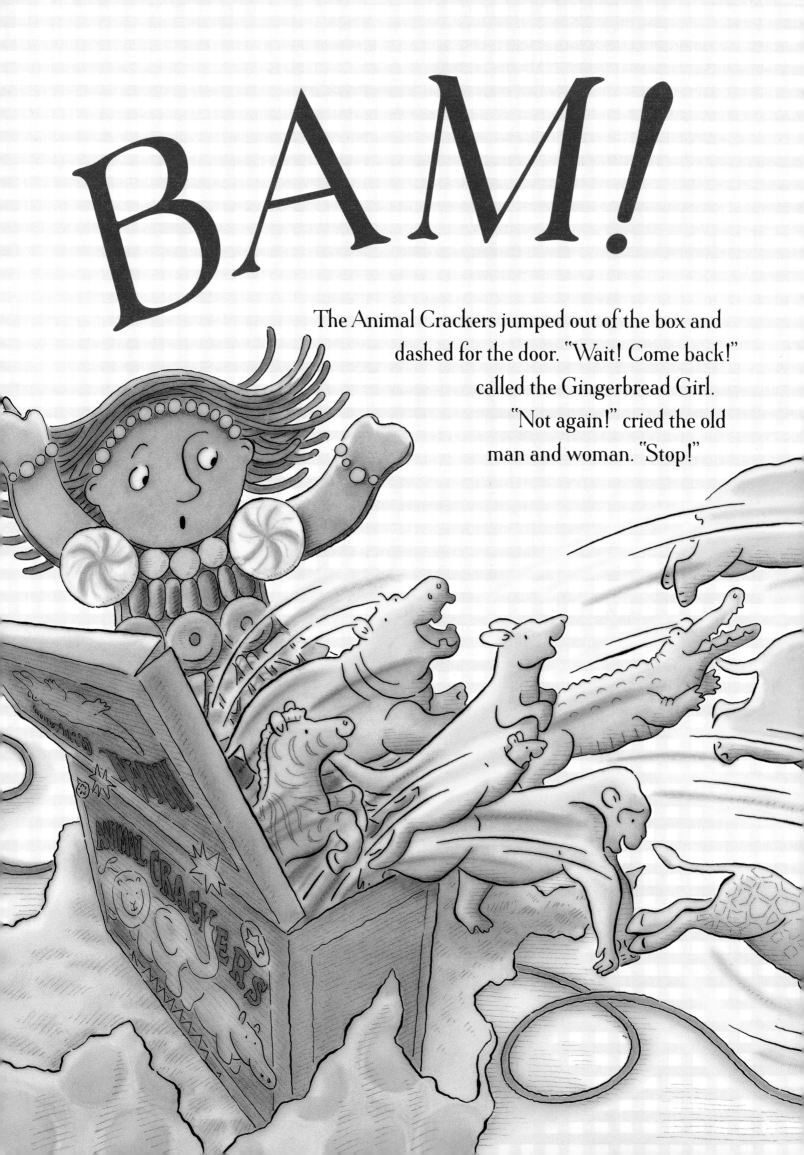

BAM!

The Animal Crackers jumped out of the box and dashed for the door. "Wait! Come back!" called the Gingerbread Girl. "Not again!" cried the old man and woman. "Stop!"

But the Animal Crackers weren't listening. They were making too much noise—the lion roared, the bear growled, the elephant trumpeted. It was cookie chaos. Animal Crackers gone wild!

As they sped out the door, they sang,

"We're wild Animal Crackers,
Hear our fierce roar.
You can't catch us,
We're off to explore!"

The Gingerbread Girl
ran after them, begging,
"Please, come back!"
  But the Animal Crackers
rushed on, raising a noisy ruckus. They
zipped past the neighboring farmers who joined the
chase as they heard,

"I'm strong and I'm fast,
Though I smell like vanilla.
You can't catch me,
I'm the cracker gorilla!"

Then the unboxed mob shouted,

"We're wild Animal Crackers,
Hear our fierce roar.

You can't catch us,
We're off to explore!"

The Gingerbread Girl ran fast, but the Animal Crackers ran faster. They shot past a cat that looked up from stalking a mouse. "Yum!" he purred, then pounced toward the crackers, catching nothing but thin air.

The mouse, too, tried for a nibble, but soon found she was running behind the whole brouhaha.

They heard a laughing voice sing,

"I'm quick and I'm noisy,
I trumpet and rant.
You can't catch me,
I'm the cracker elephant!"

And the whole gang sang again,

"We're wild Animal Crackers,
Hear our fierce roar.
You can't catch us,
We're off to explore!"

Still, the Gingerbread Girl kept running, calling, "Wait! You're headed for danger!"

The Animal Crackers continued their charge past a flock of sheep munching grass. The sheep shook their tails and bleated, "Come ba-a-a-a-a-a-ck!" joining the chase.

The sheep heard a roaring voice sing,

"My legs move so fast,
I'm practically flyin'.
You can't catch me,
I'm the wild cracker lion!"

And everyone sang,

"We're wild Animal Crackers,
Hear our fierce roar.

You can't catch us,
We're off to explore!"

The rowdy Animal Crackers raced past a group of children out flying kites. The kites swooped toward earth as the fliers turned to see the tasty beasts whiz past. "Look—cookies!" one shouted, and they soon fell in step.

Grabbing their kites, they heard,

> *"I'll whoop and I'll shout,*
> *Make a hullabaloo.*
> *You can't catch me,*
> *I'm the cracker kangaroo!"*

Then joined in the chorus,

"We're wild Animal Crackers,
Hear our fierce roar.
You can't catch us,
We're off to explore!"

Giddy with freedom, the Animal Crackers sped toward a mother hen with new baby chicks looking for bugs to eat. As the stampede approached, the chicks peeped, "Mommy! Those look *way* better than bugs!" The hen bobbed her head to claim a crunchy treat, but missed.

As the cookies made their getaway, the flustered fowls heard,

"To think you can grab me
Is oh so preposterous.
You can't catch me,
I'm the cracker rhinoceros!"

Then the unstoppable menagerie sang,

"We're wild Animal Crackers,
Hear our fierce roar.
You can't catch us,
We're off to explore!"

The Animal Crackers thundered past a scout troop
out for a hike. The scouts were tired and hungry.
"Food!" the patrol leader shouted. "Follow me, men!"
But the Animal Crackers were too quick for them,
racing on down the path.
The scouts heard a growly voice sing,

"I'll give you advice,
And that is: BEWARE!
You can't catch me,
I'm the cracker Polar Bear!"

Then a booming,

"We're wild Animal Crackers,
Hear our fierce roar.

You can't catch us, We're off to explore!"

As the Animal Crackers rounded a curve, they came face to face with a fox—the very same fox that ate the Gingerbread Boy and tried to eat the Gingerbread Girl. He sat, smiling, in front of a wide river.

The stunned cookies screeched to a halt.

"So, we're off exploring, are we?" the fox asked with a snicker. "Goodness, my little friends, we can't let a silly river stop you, can we? I have lots of experience helping cookies across. Just jump onto my tail!"

The Animal Crackers, suddenly quieter, sang,

"We're wild Animal Crackers
Just out of the box.
You won't try to eat us?
Can we trust you, Mr. Fox?"

"Of course, my sweets!" lied the
hungry fox, licking his lips.

The fox's tail was boarded like a furry Noah's ark, and he dove into the water.

"Oooooh, the water is so deep, you'd better move to my back!" the fox insisted, trying to decide whom he would eat first.

The Animal Crackers cautiously did as they were told.

"Nice," cooed the fox. "Oh my, my, my, the water is deeper now, you'd better move to my head!"

The crackers tiptoed closer.

"Stop right there!" yelled the Gingerbread Girl from the bank.

The fox turned, snarling. "Too late, candy girl—you can't stop me this time. I'm going to eat your precious friends, one tasty bite at a time!"
The shocked Animal Crackers began to cry.

But the Gingerbread Girl thought fast. "Friends, listen up! You may be little, but you're LOUD! Fox ears are supersensitive—even a tiny noise sounds huge. And an enormous noise? Look where you are!"

The Animal Crackers raced to the fox's ears as the Gingerbread Girl sang out loud and clear,

"Make a hullabaloo,
Like never before.
It's time to be noisy,
Let's hear your fierce …

The fox was a blur as he shot out of the water, trying to escape the explosive sound of the brave little crackers.

As he ran past the Gingerbread Girl, the Animal Crackers leaped to her protective embrace with more whoops and hollers.

Together, they danced back home with the crowd in tow, singing:

"We'll run and we'll run,
With a leap and a twirl.
We Animal Crackers
Love the Gingerbread GIRL!"

Her birthday cake sat waiting for a celebration of friends, old and new.

Later that night, the exhausted Animal Crackers
cuddled together, drifting to sleep with a lullaby sung
quietly by their beloved Gingerbread Girl:

"Our day has been crazy,
It's been quite a whirl.
You're safe here at last,
With your Gingerbread GIRL!"

And indeed they were.